Moonstones

Written and Illustrated by

Jan Jones

MOONSTONES

The Story of the Tooth Fairies

I had been sleepily aware of the bright shafts of light dancing across my eyelids, long before I opened my eyes. I tried in vain to ignore them, tossing and turning, wanting desperately to drift back into my comfortable dreams, but the lights danced on.

After a while I became so curious that I opened my eyes the tiniest crack, and peeped out.

There, just above the foot of my bed, bathed in pools of violet and rose light, hovered two perfect little figures. I gazed at them for what seemed like hours, watching their glow change from pink to a calmer silver-blue as they settled down onto my bed.

We studied each other silently. The fairies knew I was no longer asleep, though I hadn't moved so much as a finger, and I wondered why they didn't fly away. Instead they slowly tiptoed towards me, and then as their confidence grew, they spoke.

"I am Willow, and this is Zem," a soft gentle voice floated to my ears.

"Please help us to free Elle....Elle....Elle......" The last word hung on the air like an echo.

"It is her first tooth mission. She panicked when the boy snored, and flew behind the wardrobe to hide her light. Now she is caught and dying"

The urgency in their voices brought me to my senses, and I leapt up to hurry after the swooping figures, to where Elle hid, tangled and desperate.

I could only just reach her, and as my hand closed around the tiny figure to lift her down from the thick black cobweb, the fairy's light turned to crimson, and I was sure that she would die.

But the moment Elle felt herself free, she sped out of my grasp, spinning and tumbling wildly in her fright. Zem flew swiftly beneath her, supporting her body with his own as they spiraled down onto a pillow like dying butterflies, whilst Willow sprinkled golden dust over them both as they fell.

Then we all waited, watching Elle's light fade from crimson to rose pink as slowly, she regained her strength. It was during these waiting hours that Zem told me their story, about the Circle of Iylis,and the Ice Queen, and how they first began to collect baby teeth.

I listened wide-eyed, wondering, perhaps, if I was still dreaming. As the first light of day broke over the treetops, and they made ready to fly away with Elle, I made them a promise that sent them spinning into hoops of joy. I promised to tell their tale to the Children of the World, who the fairies love so dearly, and have wished for so long to thank. As you will read for yourself, without your precious baby teeth, the World could not survive.

THE FAIRIES' TALE

When Zem was very young, hundreds and hundreds of years ago, he served at the Court of the Circle of Iylis. It was a very happy Circle, and the most loved throughout the Fairy Kingdom.

Every evening the King and Queen held a banquet for their friends and neighbours and it was Zem's job to see that the fires were kept burning with bracken and mosses. For some weeks it seemed that the fires didn't burn as hot as usual. He fed them frantically, yet still the guests complained of the cold, and the nights grew more wintry, even though it was almost Springtime.

"It is strange," murmured the Queen one dark cool evening. "What has happened to Spring?"

Zem gathered up a thistledown shawl and wrapped it around her small white shoulders, miserable that his efforts to keep the palace warm were so useless.

"Dear Zem" she smiled, drawing him closer. "My guests are cold, will you help me to find out what is wrong?"

Zem's heart leapt to know that the Queen didn't blame him. That she should trust him with a mission was more than he could have wished,

"Fly to the North, Zem." She spoke softly, hoping not to alert the King, who never liked to make a fuss. "Ask the Ice Queen if she has seen any sign of Spring - but be careful, for the journey is long and treacherous."

Zem knew that the Ice Queen would not see him alone, and so he chose three others to accompany him. Willow would act as guide, and Tolly and Star would carry the nectar they needed for the long journey.

The palace buzzed with excitement, and they planned their speeches well into the night. Then, as the first rays of the sun touched the frozen Earth, they waxed their wings against the biting winds, and began the long journey North.

The sun shone for only an hour. The four fairies had to settle down often, cold and exhausted, hardly daring to go on for fear their brittle wings would break and send them cascading down on to the ice below. Willow and Star became weak; they were all on the point of turning back when, at last, they saw ahead of them the glacier that marked the edge of the Ice Queen's territory. They struggled on with their last breath until they reached it.

From the top of the glacier they could see the whole magnificent Ice Kingdom spread out below them. Tolly could hardly contain his excitement "Look at the Palace!" He shrieked, bouncing up and down on his frozen little feet.

The sight was splendid. The main palace stood at the centre of the Kingdom, every turret, window and door carved out of solid ice, so that it shone in the moonlight like a million diamonds. Blue and silver lights twinkled from every corner, and ice-capped towers stretched long glistening fingers way up into soft white clouds. Only Willow had breath to speak, but then she had visited the Kingdom once before when the old Queen ruled.

She looked now at the rest of the party, her voice quiet and tense.

"How can a Kingdom grow so quickly?" She whispered. "It is a hundred times bigger than I remember - the Queen must be building new palaces all the time."

They stood side by side wondering why the Ice Queen needed so many more cities to add to her already glorious Kingdom.

The silence was shattered by the most bloodcurdling scream, and the flash of ghostly white wings above them. The fairies flew together and huddled close as the great white eagle settled beside them. One sweep of his mighty talons, one snap of his hooked beak, would send all of them to their deaths. The eagle watched their slightest movement as they clung to each other , trembling.

"This is the Ice Queen's territory," the bird hissed. "What do you want?"

"We have come to speak with the Queen," Zem's voice squeaked back. The eagle rushed forward, his head tilted eagerly, his cruel eyes hungry and piercing. Zem felt his knees buckle. "On a mission from the Circle of Iylis!" he added, just as the giant bird was about to strike. At this the eagle ruffled his chest, as if uncertain what to do.

"If you eat us you'll be in trouble. Your Queen is expecting us." Zem lied

The eagle's claws closed round the four fairies, and scooped them up towards his razor beak. Then, just as they had given up all hope, they found themselves dropped into the circle of the eagle's golden crown, where they stayed like prisoners in a cage, as the great King of birds spread his wings and glided from the face of the glacier down towards the palace below.

"This is hardly the reception we expected" grumbled Tolly, as they stumbled along the slippery corridors leading to the Throne Room. "All those pretty speeches we wrote aren't going to help us much now."

"Quiet, quiet!" Yelled the guard, a nasty looking Ice Imp, who was waiting for an excuse to have them all fed to the polar bears. "Mind your manners! Speak when you are spoken to!"

They came at last to the Throne Room, a vast ice cavern, domed over with ice so thin that light flooded into every corner, blinding them all for a moment after the gloomy corridors they had recently travelled through.

"Hurry forward, hurry forward." The Ice Imp screeched, prodding each in turn with an icicle. "Don't keep the Queen waiting. She won't be kept waiting!"

At the far end of the cavern towered the Throne. As the four made their way slowly forward, they had time to gaze at the splendid sight. Flights of shimmering steps led up to the foot of the Throne, which was carved from the ice into the shape of a gigantic swan. There nestled between the curved wings, sat the Ice Queen herself, so ghostly white she could have been carved from the ice too. Only her fingers moved, long slender fingers tapering to icicles at the tips, drumming impatiently as the fairies moved towards her.

She looked down from her high Throne, with eyes as blue and cold as sapphires, her long silver hair spread around her like the finest dew-covered web. The fairies stood small and frightened at her feet, unable to utter a word.

"Who are you?" Her voice high and thin, sounded like a whisper on the breeze, and they could feel the iciness of her breath close round them as she spoke.

Zem stepped forward, remembering his speech. "We are messengers, sent from the Circle of Iylis," he began. "My Queen wishes to know if you, your Majesty, have seen any sign of Spring."

"Spring!" The Queen's voice cracked, and she rose to her feet enraged. "Spring will NEVER come!" She turned her beautiful face towards them. "I have forbidden it !"

"But why?" Star in her surprise quite forgot herself "Why?"

"Because she melts my Kingdom every time she passes. My Kingdom must stand forever. I will not have Spring near my Kingdom!" The Queen in her rage blew blasts of cold air that froze the sentries to their posts, and chilled the fairies to the bone.

"But the Earth has grown cold, and everything on it will die, unless you allow Spring to come," Star pleaded.

"Tell your Circle of Iylis" howled the Ice Queen, "that the Earth can freeze over for all I care. My Kingdom will stand, it will stand higher and longer than the Snow Queen's, who boasts so freely about her crystal turrets and snow-capped mountains" she spun around angrily, pointing her long icicled finger towards Zem "Have you ever, in any corner of the Earth, seen a sight that can outshine my Kingdom?"

Zem was lost for an answer. Willow and Star began to weep, remembering the sight that had met their eyes when they looked from the top of the glacier; the million diamonds, twinkling stars; only the moon had shone brighter…...……..the MOON! Zem's heart missed a beat.

"Yes your Majesty." His voice quavered now, as he struggled to keep calm. "The Moon shines brighter than your Kingdom."

The Queen froze, and he wondered for a moment if she had turned to ice. Only her eyes flashed over him as he waited.

"It is true, the Moon shines brightest." She spoke at last. "If I could build my Kingdom with stones from the Moon the Snow Queen would turn green with envy."

"We will bring them to you, I promise!" Zem rushed towards the Throne, afraid to miss the only chance left to him. "We will build you a Kingdom from the Moon. It will outshine every Kingdom imaginable; not even Spring could destroy it - the stones will be strong enough to last for eternity."

The Queen was far to proud and vain to resist. She bowed her head and stretched her arms wide.

"If you can do this for me," she sighed, "then Spring will be yours again for ever."

Zem didn't know how he could keep his promise, but it was the only hope of bringing Spring back to the Earth, and a way must be found.

The fairies left the cavern with the sound of the Queen's tinkling laughter ringing in their ears, knowing the impossible task they had set for themselves.

The Court of Iylis grew silent as Zem told of the meeting with the Ice Queen. Even the busy scribes dropped their quills, forgetting their duties, as they listened. The King and Queen gazed at each other helplessly, and when the story was told, it was many minutes before anyone spoke a word.

" It is impossible," the King broke the silence, "none of us could reach the Moon......send for Aley."

The wise old owl shuffled into the Court, his spectacles perched on the tip of his beak, his feathers ruffled from being rushed away from his studies. He was the wisest of all the King's advisers, and the only one to turn to in a crisis. He slammed a pile of books down on to the bench, and flicked open a page.

"My calculations tell me," he muttered, more to himself than to the Court, "that man will not fly to the Moon for hundreds of years, so there is little hope of us achieving it sooner. No, the answer lies elsewhere. We must cheat.

Cheat! It was a terrible thought, and the whole Court rose in disorder, but the old bird continued as if he hadn't noticed

"To save the Earth from certain destruction, we must tell the Ice Queen a little white lie." The Court began to listen again.

"We must find a gem to build her palaces, and tell her it has come from the Moon."

"What on Earth can ever compare with Moonstones?" The Queen interrupted. "All the diamonds in the entire Fairy World wouldn't be enough to build a Kingdom, even if we tried."

The owl held up his wing.

We must send for those who understand gems, those and everyone else's......send for the thieving magpies."

A gasp went up in the hushed Court. The magpies had been banished from Court long ago; they stole anything that glittered, and hoarded it away in their nests until these bulged like overstuffed treasure chests. They had never been popular at Court, but when they stole the Iysil crown they were banished for ever. To bring them back now, in the Circle's hour of need, was more than the King could bear.

"Those thieves and vagabonds, I will not have them in my Court!" Yelled the King.

Zem stepped forward nervously. "Will you allow me to go to the magpies, your Majesty? I knew one of them once; they are not really so bad when you get to know them."

The Queen came to the rescue

"MY dear, what a wonderful idea. If Zem will travel to the magpie colony, our problem is solved.

And so it was, at first light of day, that the four fairies set out again, this time to find the magpies. It wasn't as difficult as they had imagined; since their exile the King had ordered the magpies to wear flashes of white on their wing and chest feathers, as a warning to others of their misdeeds. So by the time the fairies approached the colony the magpies could clearly be seen as they swooped from tree to tree, storing their treasure and plotting more mischief.

They in turn spotted the fairies as they settled on a mossy root, and amused the four by scurrying to and fro, covering their treasure with leaves, and putting on an air of innocence.

"Well what a surprise," said the chief, slightly out of breath and flustered. "The boys were just having a little tidy out, you know," he added, pushing a shiny object out of sight. "To what do we owe the pleasure?"

"We've come to hunt through your treasure, if you'll allow us," Willow blurted, keen to see the hoards of trinkets.

"Packed all that in a long time ago," said the crafty bird, "Going straight we are."

"A magpie doesn't change his flashes so quickly, " Zem smiled. "For once we would be glad to see your treasure trove. There is a pardon from the King if you will help us."

The bird whistled through his beak. "A pardon you say What can we do to help? Say the word."

At that the magpies flew up and unmasked pile after pile of glittering objects. "Take your pick, master; a lovely emerald brooch here for the Queen, or how about a ruby necklace?"

They searched for hours amongst the treasure, but nothing looked remotely like a stone from the Moon.

The magpies were in despair, presenting their finest gold and silver, and every coloured gem imaginable.

Zem lifted the last ring from the very last nest left to search, when something beneath it caught his eye. There, shining brightly between the thorns and mosses, lay the nearest thing to a Moonstone he had ever hoped to find.

"What is this?" Zem lifted the tiny stone from the nest triumphantly, as the others crowded around.

"That's it!" Shouted Tolly. "We've found it!"

"That!" Screeched the chief. That's nothing! Now let me show you this……."

"We want this one," Zem insisted, "What is it?"

"It's a tooth," blinked the chief, hardly able to believe his ears. "One of the young ones brought it back, didn't know what was what, do you see. Thought because it shone it was valuable, but it's not, it's not!"

"Never mind, this is the one. Can you tell us where to find more like it?"

"Well of course," the bird puffed out his chest. "That's easy there are millions of them. Humans leave them about all over the place."

The fairies could hardly believe their luck. To find a Moonstone was one thing, but to know there were millions more was sheer joy. They left the magpies, still dazed by their good fortune

"That's all you want?" Asked the chief over and over again. "And we can keep our treasure, and the Royal pardon?"

As the fairies swooped overhead with their precious cargo, the magpies were busily packing their stolen loot back into hiding, squabbling and fighting over every object. Only the chief watched the fairies go, his head on one side and a puzzled expression in his eye.

18.

There was no time to lose. Already the Earth, so long without the sun, had begun to freeze; the trees stayed bare of leaves, and the birds and animals disappeared into their homes, as if they knew the winter would last forever.

The whole Circle of Iylis left their duties for the tooth missions, and it was decided that small groups of three or four would search every house in the Kingdom. The magpies, now the heroes of the Circle, accompanied each group for the first time, showing them where to look for the precious teeth, and teaching each one not to be hasty, but to wait until they were certain that the children were asleep.

"Take your time," nodded the magpie chief as the four alighted on the first window-sill. "They may look harmless asleep," he added, "But I have seen sweet curly-headed angels like him pull wings off butterflies and moths. Think what he might do if he got hold of you."

Their blood ran cold. Willow had seen a Human once before, long ago, but Tolly and Star, like Zem, had only heard tales, told by the old ones; dreadful tales of fairies being chased by Humans with nets, and they had heard about the butterfly wings many times before.

"Now." Urged the old chief, "slip through that gap there, but don't be long." Tolly and Zem swooped in, and hovered briefly over the sleeping figure. They could see his soft golden curls above the coverlet, and the tip of his shiny little nose. It was difficult now to believe that he would harm them if he woke.

"Hurry, Zem," Tolly motioned towards his wings, where he had wrapped the silver net ready to carry the tooth away. He slung the net between them, and carefully lifted the tooth until it was safely enmeshed, then, with no hesitation, sped back towards the gap in the window, and safety.

"You were wonderful" Laughed Willow and Star, wrapping their arms around the heroes' necks.

"Couldn't have stolen it better myself." Chuckled the old chief.

His words stopped Zem in his tracks."The coin, we have forgotten the coin!" Aley, the wise old owl, had assured the Court that if the fairies left something of value for the children, in place of the tooth, then they would not be stealing but simply exchanging. Now in his panic, Zem had forgotten to leave the little coin that children value so much. Willow mischievously produced the missing coin from the foxglove bell she carried around her waist.

"Our turn next." She winked happily, as she and Star flew deftly through the gap, and laid the coin down gently on the child's pillow.

The Human children soon began to realise that their teeth were being exchanged during the night for a coin, and happily left their teeth especially for the fairies, well within reach.

Sometimes the tooth gleamed temptingly on a bedside table, sometimes it was tucked out of sight under a pillow. The fairies grew braver and more daring with each mission, but they had the magpies to remind them now and again about the butterfly wings

By the next full Moon enough baby teeth had been collected to build the palace. The fairy craftsmen worked day and night, shaping and polishing the little teeth so that they fitted together perfectly. They cut shapes for the high arched windows, and chiseled petal edges for the roofs. Some they carved into flowers and animals to decorate the doors and eaves, but the most delicate of all were the hundreds of water-spouts, carved into the likeness of the children all over the Earth, who had given their teeth to the fairies.

One evening, as Zem was tending the fires, the King and Queen called him to them.

"Zem, you have done so much for us already, that what I have to ask…………." The Queen looked away blushing.

"My Queen," he replied "to serve you and the Circle of Iylis is all I live for. Whatever you ask of me, I am honoured to obey."

"Zem, we must ask you again to travel to the North. The Ice Queen has heard of our progress, and she grows impatient. She is sending her Snow Geese to bring the Moonstones back to the Ice Kingdom; she will wait no longer."

They could do no more; every Moonstone was carved and shaped ready, and now the moment had come to confront the Ice Queen

And so, a week later, the precious cargo of Moonstones was loaded carefully on to the backs of the Snow Geese, and the fairies set off, with the craftsmen, on the perilous journey North.

The same white eagle greeted them as they approached the Ice Queen's territory, but they noticed that he was far more polite than the last time they'd met. He guided the party over the glacier and down into the Kingdom, where the fairies unloaded the Moonstones and watched sadly as the Snow Geese gaggled away into the darkness, leaving them alone and frozen from the long journey

"The Queen will not see you until the Moon Palace is finished," rasped the eagle; then, without waiting for an answer, he spread his gigantic wings and soared away.

The fairies worked without food or sleep; their limbs became so cold that they could hardly lift the Moonstones, and the flights to the topmost turrets were becoming more and more difficult as their wings iced over. But the palace grew, slowly at first, and then faster as they became desperate and used their fairy magic, until at last the Moon Palace was complete.

The fairies stood in amazement at the magnificent sight. None of them was prepared for such a victory. They had dreamed of course, of how it might look, but even in their wildest dreams they couldn't have imagined the sheer beauty of the palace.

It shone twice as brightly as the Moon; every smooth white surface glistened like pearls. The old Ice Palace, that they had once thought so wonderful, now looked pale and watery against the rich ivory gleam of the Moon Palace.

All around the birds and animals gathered, wondering what was causing such a glow.

"Has the Moon fallen?" Asked a nasty little Ice Imp. "I must tell the Queen"

Suddenly they heard a crack, like a whiplash, as the mighty Ice Palace doors opened, and the Ice Queen glided slowly towards them.

"Your Majesty," they all bowed low, "your gift from the Circle of Iylis." Zem stepped back, and as the Queen approached she spread her arms wide in wonder at the sight.

"This is indeed carved from the Moon itself!" She gasped, and glided around her Moon Palace, delighting in every tiny detail. She was clearly very happy.

They danced until dawn. Everyone in the Ice Kingdom joined in the celebrations. The craftsmen were the guests of honour, dancing and feasting until everyone thought they would burst, and even the white eagle came down from his lofty perch to join in the fun. It was the happiest night anyone could remember.

Spring came the next morning, and every creature basked in the sunlight as the gentle rays melted the old Ice Kingdom, and travelled on South towards Iylis and the waiting World.

The Ice Queen still believes that her palace is made of Moonstones, and to this day the fairies continue to collect baby teeth, for without them the palaces would fall into ruins.

The Circle of Iylis is as happy as ever, though now they are known far and wide as the Tooth Fairies.

Their mission is important, for as long as children leave their precious baby teeth for them to find, the Ice Queen will be happy, and the World will always be able to say,

"Winter won't last forever..............Spring will soon be here"

Printed in Great Britain
by Amazon